Dear Parents and Educators,

Welcome to Penguin Young Readers! As parents and educators, you know that each child develops at his or her own pace—in terms of speech, critical thinking, and, of course, reading. Penguin Young Readers recognizes this fact. As a result, each Penguin Young Readers book is assigned a traditional easy-to-read level (1–4) as well as a Guided Reading Level (A–P). Both of these systems will help you choose the right book for your child. Please refer to the back of each book for specific leveling information. Penguin Young Readers features esteemed authors and illustrators, stories about favorite characters, fascinating nonfiction, and more!

Kate Skates

LEVEL **2**

GUIDED READING LEVEL **F**

This book is perfect for a **Progressing Reader** who:
- can figure out unknown words by using picture and context clues;
- can recognize beginning, middle, and ending sounds;
- can make and confirm predictions about what will happen in the text; and
- can distinguish between fiction and nonfiction.

Here are some **activities** you can do during and after reading this book:
- Read the Pictures: Use the pictures to tell the story. Have the child go through the book, retelling the story just by looking at the pictures.
- Make Connections: In this story, Kate looks up to Diana Lin, a famous ice-skater. Diana Lin is Kate's role model. A role model is someone who sets a good example for others. Is there someone you look up to? Who is it and why? What makes them a good role model?

Remember, sharing the love of reading with a child is the best gift you can give!

—Bonnie Bader, EdM
  Penguin Young Readers program

*Penguin Young Readers are leveled by independent reviewers applying the standards developed by Irene Fountas and Gay Su Pinnell in *Matching Books to Readers: Using Leveled Books in Guided Reading*, Heinemann, 1999.

For Mom, who is also a terrific grandma.
With love—JOC

To all great beginners—DD

Penguin Young Readers
Published by the Penguin Group
Penguin Group (USA) Inc., 375 Hudson Street, New York, New York 10014, USA
Penguin Group (Canada), 90 Eglinton Avenue East, Suite 700, Toronto, Ontario M4P 2Y3, Canada
(a division of Pearson Penguin Canada Inc.)
Penguin Books Ltd, 80 Strand, London WC2R 0RL, England
Penguin Ireland, 25 St Stephen's Green, Dublin 2, Ireland (a division of Penguin Books Ltd)
Penguin Group (Australia), 707 Collins Street, Melbourne, Victoria 3008, Australia
(a division of Pearson Australia Group Pty Ltd)
Penguin Books India Pvt Ltd, 11 Community Centre, Panchsheel Park, New Delhi—110 017, India
Penguin Group (NZ), 67 Apollo Drive, Rosedale, Auckland 0632, New Zealand
(a division of Pearson New Zealand Ltd)
Penguin Books (South Africa), Rosebank Office Park, 181 Jan Smuts Avenue,
Parktown North 2193, South Africa
Penguin China, B7 Jiaming Center, 27 East Third Ring Road North,
Chaoyang District, Beijing 100020, China

Penguin Books Ltd, Registered Offices: 80 Strand, London WC2R 0RL, England

Text copyright © 1995 by Jane O'Connor. Illustrations copyright © 1995 by DyAnne DiSalvo.
All rights reserved. First published in 1995 by Grosset & Dunlap, an imprint of Penguin Group (USA) Inc.
Published in 2013 by Penguin Young Readers, an imprint of Penguin Group (USA) Inc.,
345 Hudson Street, New York, New York 10014. Manufactured in China.

Library of Congress Control Number: 94045101

ISBN 978-0-448-40935-1   10 9 8 7 6 5 4 3

Kate Skates

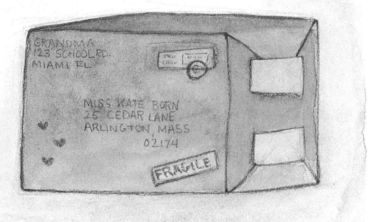

by Jane O'Connor
illustrated by DyAnne DiSalvo

Penguin Young Readers
An Imprint of Penguin Group (USA) Inc.

I am so happy today.

I just got new skates.

They are for big kids.

They have only one blade.

Grandma sent them

for my birthday.

My sister is happy, too.

She is happy because

she has my old skates.

Grandma also sent a little skirt.

Now I look like

the skaters on TV.

"Let's go," I tell my little sister.

"Let's try our skates."

Now my little sister

does not look so happy.

"I do not know how to skate,"

Jen says.

But I tell her not to worry.

I will show Jen

how to skate.

That is what

big sisters are for.

Mom takes us to the rink.

"Oh look!" I say.

"Diana Lin is coming here."

I have seen Diana Lin

on TV lots of times.

I want to skate like her

someday.

My little sister and I

put on our skates.

It does not take Jen long.

It takes me longer.

"I am coming, Jen,"

I tell her.

"Do not be scared.

I will hold your hand.

I will help you . . ."

11

But my little sister

does not need help.

"This is fun,"

she says.

"Come on, Kate."

I walk to the rail.

My skates look so cool.

My skirt looks so cool.

I can't wait to skate.

Right away

I find out something.

My new skates

are harder

than my old skates—

much harder.

I slip.

I wobble.

A big kid crashes

into me.

There is only one thing

I am good at—

falling!

I fall lots of times.

I do not look at all

like the skaters on TV.

I see a big kid laughing.

I am glad when it is time to go.

A week later,

we go back to the rink.

I try skating again.

And do you know what?

I am not as bad as the last time.

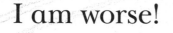

I am worse!

"Hold my hand.

I will help you," Jen tells me.

She is being nice.

But *she* is the little sister.

I am the big sister.

I do not want her help.

All of a sudden, it gets noisy.

Diana Lin will skate soon.

Great!

Now everybody has to

get off the ice.

Great again!

I am sick of skating.

But Jen wants to go around

one more time.

Jen skates away.

She is out pretty far.

She does not see

a big kid coming.

Oh no!

He is going to crash

into her.

"Jen! Watch out!" I yell.

I wobble out to help her.

That is what big sisters are for.

I pull her out of the way.

But now I cannot stop.

I spin around and around

like a top.

Then I crash into somebody.

Down I go!

"Here.

Let me help you."

I look up.

It is a pretty girl

in a pretty dress.

I have seen her on TV

lots of times.

It is Diana Lin!

Diana Lin smiles.

"That was some spin!"

But I shake my head.

"It was not on purpose.

I can't skate."

"I bet you just need some help.

After my show,

I can help you.

Deal?"

Is she kidding?

Me and Diana Lin!

"Deal!" I say.

I watch Diana Lin.

She can jump . . .

and spin

on purpose.

Wow!

Is she good!

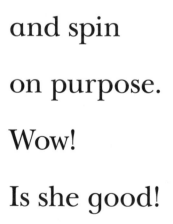

28

Then Diana Lin

comes over to me.

She holds out her hands.

I am scared.

Everybody is looking.

What if they laugh

like that big kid?

But I take her hands.

She shows me

how to push and glide.

It is like Diana Lin is

my big sister.

Around the rink we go.

Push, push, glide.

And do you know what?

I am not as bad as before.

I get better!

I even let go of her hands

for a little.

I am skating on big-kid skates!

That night,

Diana Lin is on the TV news.

And do you know what?

So am I!

Maybe I will be as good as

Diana Lin . . . someday!